QED Read On

Going to School

Sally Hewitt

QED Publishing

First published in the UK in 2005 by
QED Publishing
A Quarto Group company
226 City Road
London EC1V 2TT
www.qed-publishing.co.uk

A Catalogue record for this book is available from the British Library.

ISBN 1 84538 174 2

Written by Sally Hewitt
Designed by Zeta Jones
Editor Hannah Ray
Picture Researcher Nic Dean

Series Consultant Anne Faundez
Publisher Steve Evans
Creative Director Louise Morley
Editorial Manager Jean Coppendale

Printed and bound in China

Picture credits

Key: t = top, b = bottom, m = middle, l = left, r = right

Alamy Images/Greenshoots Communications 7, 19t, 22m /Paul Doyle 9t, 20t;
Corbis/Julie Habel 5, 18t, /Peter Turnley 8, 19b, /Gabe Palmer 9b, 22t, /Dave G.
Houser 10, /Paul A. Sauders 12, 21t, /Galen Rowell 13, Tom & Dee Ann McCarthy 14,
/Steve Raymer 15; **Getty Images**/David Lees/Taxi 4, /Tony Arruza/Stone 11t, 20b,
/Mel Yates/Taxi 11b, /Mark Lewis/Stone 16, 21b, /Paul Chelsey/Stone 17, 22b; **Still
Pictures**/Ron Giling 6, 18b.

Contents

Going to school

It's a school day in St Paul,
Minnesota, in the USA.
Martha and her sister wait
for the yellow school bus.

They say "good morning"
to the driver and go and sit
with their friends.

The children talk
and laugh all the
way to school.

My school

Kwame's school in Ghana is surrounded by trees and farmland. He walks six and a half kilometres to school with his friends.

The school walls are made of concrete.
The roof is **corrugated iron**.

Sometimes, Kwame has lessons outside,
in the shade of a big tree.

Learning to read

All over the world, children learn how to read their own language. Farouk is learning how to read and write Arabic.

Anja is from Sweden.

She is blind, so she is learning to read words that are written in **Braille**.

She feels the words with her fingers.

Games and PE

Wesley's school is in Trinidad, in the West Indies. His favourite game is cricket. One day, he wants to play in the school cricket team.

Sarah is learning to play basketball at her school in Birmingham, in England.

She can run fast and shoot goals.

School clothes

Chen, Li and Shaiming all go to school together in Beijing, China.

They look very smart in their school uniform.

Nanook and Sedna wear warm
clothes to go to school.

It is cold in Alaska,
in North America,
where they live.

Playtime

In fine weather, children play outside at playtime.

Caitlin and her friends love climbing the ropes in her school playground in Toronto, Canada.

14

Chi, Kim and Yen take their skipping ropes
to school in Danang, Vietnam. They have
great fun at playtime! Everyone lines up
to have a go.

The school show

Putri's parents have come to see her dance in the school show.

Putri has learned a **traditional** Indonesian dance.

Putri's mother remembers learning the same dance when she was at school.

What do you think?

Why do you think bright yellow is a good colour for a school bus?

Can you remember how Kwame gets to school every day?

18

Can you describe
Kwame's school?
How is it different
from yours?

What language
is Farouk
learning to read
and write?

19

Why does Anja
use her
fingers
to read?

What is Wesley's
favourite game?
Do you know
how to play it?

How can you tell Chen, Li and Shaiming go to the same school?

What have Putri's parents come to see at the school show?

Glossary

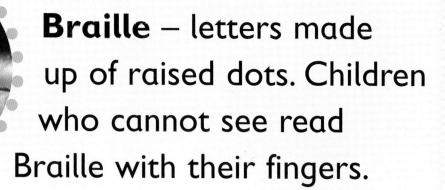

Braille – letters made up of raised dots. Children who cannot see read Braille with their fingers.

Corrugated iron – a thin sheet of iron bent into waves to make it stronger.

Traditional – dances or stories from the past that parents teach to their children.

Index

23

Parents' and teachers' notes

- Look at the cover of the book together. Talk about how the picture gives us an idea of what is inside the book.
- Read the title. Explain that the title tells us what the book is about.
- Explain that this is a non-fiction book, which gives us facts and information. Talk about the difference between fiction, which tells a story, and non-fiction.
- Read the book together, discussing the photographs as you read each page. What extra information do the photographs give the reader?
- Spend time talking about the answers to the questions on pages 18–21. Take the opportunity to look back through the book and check your answers.
- Identify the contents page, the glossary and the index.
- Look at the contents page. Point out that it shows the different sections of the book in the order that they appear. Use the contents page to look up the page 'Learning to read'.

- Point out that the index is in alphabetical order. Explain that the index tells us where in the book we can find certain information. Use the index to look up the references to 'playtime'.
- Find the words in **bold** type and look them up in the glossary.
- Talk about how children all over the world travel to school. Help your child to draw a simple map of their route from home to school.
- Use an atlas or a globe to find the countries mentioned in the book. Identify the country where you live.
- Ask your child to tell you about his or her school day. Talk about how it might be different from Kwame's school day in Ghana.
- Together, choose one of the children in the book. Help your child to write a letter telling the chosen child about his/her school day. Your child could draw a picture of his or her school, classroom, teacher or classmates to illustrate the letter.